DATE DUE

W9-CSI-768

the
IGNORANT
monkeys

the
ignorant
monkeys
and other tales
from india

WRITTEN AND ILLUSTRATED BY

sal friscia

PANTHEON BOOKS

J
398

Copyright © 1971 by Salvatore Friscia
All rights reserved under International and Pan-American Copyright Conventions.
Published in the United States by Pantheon Books,
a division of Random House, Inc., and simultaneously in Canada
by Random House of Canada Limited, Toronto.
Trade Edition: ISBN: 0-394-82319-2
Library Edition: ISBN: 0-394-92319-7

Library of Congress Catalog Card Number: 75-153977
Manufactured in the United States of America
Typography by Harriett Banner

TO
Nina, Deirdre, Alison,
and Lisa

c.1

·THE GOOD COOK·

two *sadhus*, or holy men, wanted to go to the holy city of Bhubaneshwar. Since they had no money they were obliged to walk and beg for their food along the way. It was getting late and their rice bowls were empty when they passed a large and prosperous-looking house.

"This must be the house of a very rich man," said Hari, the elder of the two. "Let us stop and ask the owner, there, for something to eat."

"Kind sir," Hari began, "would you help two *sadhus* who are on their way to the temple at Bhubaneshwar? We have eaten nothing all day."

"Your request could not have come at a better time," replied the owner, "for I have just received some good news concerning business. There is no better way to show thanks to the gods than by helping two holy men. Tell me, what would you do with a gift of a few *rupees?*"

"Simple," replied Hari. "I would go to that shop down the road, buy some rice, a few vegetables, a bit of curry, make a fire, and cook us a delicious meal. As a treat, I might also get a sweet thing of curds and honey."

"Excellent," said the owner. "But there are two of you. Perhaps your companion has a different idea."

"Oh no," said the younger *sadhu*. "I would give him the money."

"I don't understand," said the owner.

"Easy enough," laughed the younger *sadhu*. "My friend is a much better cook than I am."

· THE GUIDE ·

a young merchant had just arrived in the ancient holy city of Benares on the banks of the Ganges River. First he went to one of the many temples to make an offering, and then struck out for the marketplace to buy some of the city's famous silks. Being unfamiliar with the narrow, winding streets, he soon was lost. As he stood wondering what to do, a young boy came up to him and asked if he could be of help.

"You certainly can," the merchant said eagerly. "Lead me to that part of the market where silks are sold and I shall reward you with a few *annas*."

"Oh, that will be easy," said the boy. "Follow me."

So off they went. Up and down steps, around temples, past courtyards, under arches, through narrow lanes, and finally into a wide street full of shops displaying gorgeous silks.

Pointing to one of them the boy said, "Here is the shop where my mother gets all of her silks—my sisters, and relatives too. Why don't you try it?"

"Not a bad idea," said the merchant.

Once inside, he made a great many purchases and spent quite a lot of money.

"This is a fine shop you have taken me to," he said to the boy as he made ready to leave. "Here are the *annas* I promised you, together with my thanks."

"Oh, don't thank me," answered the boy. "Thank my father. It's his shop."

· RAZIA ·

Razia, a little Moslem girl, was playing in the courtyard of her house in Kashmir, when her mother called. "Little one, we are going to town this morning. Wash your face and wear your new *burqua*."

Razia felt particularly lazy that day.

"I'll pretend I've washed," she decided, thinking her mother would never know she hadn't once she put on the *burqua,* which covered her from head to toe with only little openings in the hood for her eyes.

Running to her mother she said, "I am ready, let's go."

"Did you wash your face, as I asked you?"

"Oh, yes," fibbed Razia.

"Let me see your hands," demanded her mother.

Razia stuck out her hands from under the *burqua.* They were not very clean.

"What a clever little daughter I have," laughed her mother. "She can wash her face without even wetting her hands."

On the following day, he again visited the temple, and when he left he was met by the same hungry cries of *"Bakshish! Bakshish!"*

He took out his purse once more, but pausing, turned to an old beggar in rags and asked, "Did I not give you something yesterday?"

"That is true, sir," the beggar answered humbly. "I remember it well. It is my stomach which has such a poor memory."

·WAS IT MAGIC?·

a venerable holy man lived and meditated in a secluded coconut grove. His only possessions were an orange robe, a string of sacred beads, a mat, and a bowl with which to beg his food. So quietly did he sit, that birds often perched on his head and even pulled out strands of his hair to line their nests.

One day a stranger was passing through the grove. Seeing the holy man deep in meditation surrounded by so many beautiful birds, he thought to himself, "Those birds are practically tame. How simple it would be to catch them while the old fool is in a trance. They will bring a good price in the market."

He fashioned a makeshift net and was just about to throw it over the birds when a coconut dropped from a tree and landed right on his head. It knocked him senseless to the ground.

When he came to, nothing had changed in the grove. The holy man's eyes were still closed and the birds fluttered about him. The stranger rose slowly and began to back out of the grove, rubbing the bump on his head which hurt terribly. "The birds in this grove are truly ferocious," he muttered. "It would have been easier to catch a tiger."

And if you looked very closely, you could see the beginning of a smile on the holy man's face.

Pushpa had only been married a short time, but she was already proving to be a troublesome wife. Each day she would demand some new gift from her husband.

In the morning she might begin, "Tonight, bring me a bracelet like the one Mrs. Mehta has, only in gold." Or, "I have seen some lovely toe rings at the jewelers, do get me some." She might whine, "My *saris* are old" (which they were not), "I'm ashamed to visit anyone. Bring me one in dark green with lots of gold embroidery. Other husbands dress their wives decently."

Her husband did his best, but there was no pleasing Pushpa. He was beside himself. Now he had to work twice as hard to provide all the money for these luxuries, and the effort was wearing him out. He was so worried about getting into debt that he could not sleep nights, and he felt his health and zest for life leaving him. Finally he decided on a plan.

One evening he returned home with a package which his wife snatched from his hands without even a thank you. Tearing off the wrapping, she held up a white *sari,* crying in disbelief, "What is this? Surely you have made some mistake. Only widows wear this kind of *sari*!"

"No, I have made no mistake," said her husband, "for if you continue in your selfish ways, I don't expect to last much longer and you will have ample use for it."

·LORD SHIVA'S SHRINE·

a group of *sadhus* were about to begin their
annual pilgrimage to Lord Shiva's shrine
high in the mountains of Kashmir. Ahead of them
was an arduous three-day journey during which
they would endure many hardships.

As they gathered their meager possessions, one
sadhu said, "Tonight we will be in the mountains
where the winds are bitter. At first it bothered me,
but years have passed and now I simply fix my mind
on Lord Shiva and the cold does not exist for me."

Another *sadhu* spoke up. "I too have made this
pilgrimage many times. In the beginning the cold
went right through me. But I have learned to place
my thoughts and body with Lord Shiva and now it
matters not how cold it is."

The other *sadhus* nodded their heads in agreement, except for a young fellow whose beard was not very thick or long. He held up a blanket for all to see. "This is my first visit to Lord Shiva's shrine," he exclaimed. "I have no experience, and in place of it I have brought this blanket."

·THE IGNORANT MONKEYS·

Prem had just moved from New Delhi, where they speak Urdu, to Calcutta, where Bengali is spoken. Returning home from the marketplace, he put down his shopping bags near a window and left the room for a moment. The tips of some ripe yellow bananas were poking out of one of the bags, and in a twinkling, some sharp-eyed monkeys swung down to the open window and helped themselves to their favorite fruit. When Prem returned and saw them chattering and enjoying his bananas on a nearby rooftop, he flew into a rage.

"Oh, you robbers. You spiteful thieves. May the gods punish you. May you remain monkeys for all eternity." He was very angry.

Hearing all the commotion, his wife came into the room. When she saw what had happened, she said to her husband with a smile, "Prem, don't blame the monkeys for your carelessness—they were hungry. Besides, you are wasting your breath. They don't understand one word of Urdu!"

·CHICKEN CURRY·

Young Mohan stole to an out-of-the-way Moslem restaurant where he could eat meat, a food strictly forbidden by his Hindu religion.

He had just finished a savory lunch of chicken curry when—to his horror—he saw his stern and devout uncle entering the restaurant.

"I am found out," he moaned, frantically searching for some place to hide. "What shall I do?"

But his uncle didn't even notice him, and took a table to one side. Mohan could hardly believe his ears when he heard his uncle ask the waiter to bring him some lamb curry. Recovering from his fright, Mohan quickly paid his bill and stood up to leave. It was then his uncle caught sight of him.

"Oh, ah, Nephew," he stammered guiltily. "What are you doing here?"

"I have just come in for a glass of tea," said Mohan with a smile. Then going out the door he added, "You really should try the chicken curry sometime, Uncle. I understand it is excellent here."

·MORE THAN HE BARGAINED FOR·

In India, where bargaining is an art, a man shouted to a porter, "Here, take this baggage to the Madras train and I'll give you twelve *annas*."

The porter examined the baggage. "Let me see," he muttered. "A bedroll, water jug, brass pot, foot locker, bag, and umbrella. You need at least two porters. But, perhaps I can manage...if you pay me twenty *annas*."

"Two porters! Twenty *annas*!" shouted the man indignantly. "Here, let me lighten the load," he said, removing the umbrella.

The porter stared at him. "You had better open that umbrella if you know what is good for you. I am *really* going to lighten the load." And with that, he emptied the jug of water right on the man's head.

·THE ABANDONED TEMPLE·

a bearded *sadhu* stood at the side of a road, examining an old, abandoned temple that was overgrown with trees and bushes. A farmer from a nearby village saw him and stopped to chat.

"Where do you come from?" asked the farmer.

"Oh, I have been traveling from holy place to holy place," replied the *sadhu*, "and now I would like to rest for a while. I have been thinking that this temple would be the perfect place for me to spend a few quiet months."

The villager shook his head. "You can't," he told the *sadhu*. "You will lose your life. This temple is infested with poisonous snakes."

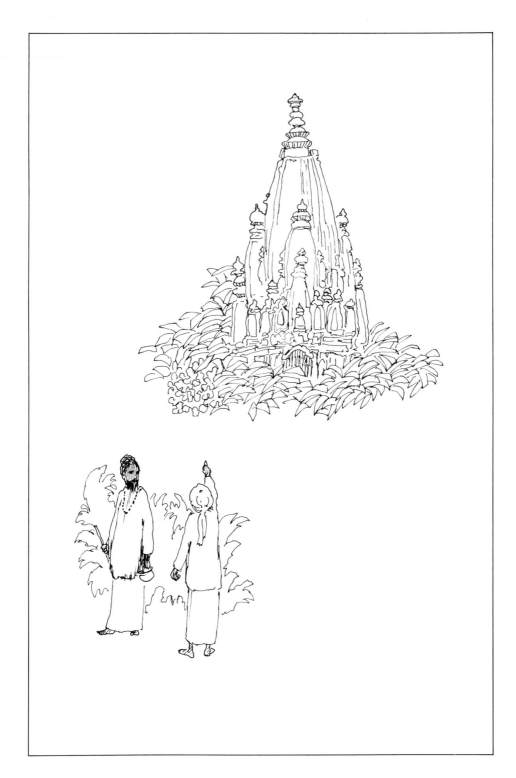

"It matters not," said the *sadhu* with a smile. "My master taught me a powerful chant which will drive the snakes out of the temple into the fields where they belong."

"No, no!" cried the villager in a horrified voice. "You mustn't do that! Only last month we paid a *sadhu* such as you to rid our fields of those very same snakes."

·A PRAYER TO GANESH·

There was a Hindu who was very careful with his money. As he was about to begin a new and daring business venture, he decided first to pray to the god Ganesh, remover of obstacles and bringer of good fortune. Turning down a narrow street, he located the shop of a well-known incense seller, and went up to the owner.

"I'm going to pray to Ganesh for good fortune, and I'd like a packet of incense to offer with my prayers."

The shopkeeper reached behind him, and taking a strong, fragrant packet from a special place, handed it over. "This will please Ganesh, I am sure. And it's only three *rupees*."

The man made a face when he heard the price. "I don't want to seem stingy," he whined, "but don't you have something a little cheaper?"

"Of course," smiled the shopkeeper, for he knew his man. "Here is a packet for one *rupee*. But I advise you, don't complain if Ganesh seems stingy with you."

·THE COBRA IN THE BASKET·

a hooded cobra, tired of his ordinary life in the jungle, left home to seek fame and fortune.

After some days of traveling, he arrived at the house of a famous snake charmer, whom he had heard praised by other cobras.

"I want to become famous," he said to the old man. "Teach me to coil and uncoil, wind and unwind, and sway from side to side to the music of your flute."

"Very well," said the snake charmer, impressed by this speech. "Remain with me, and I shall teach you all that I know."

Weeks passed and the cobra proved himself quick to learn. One morning the old man said to him, "Get into that basket and we'll go to the city and give our first performance, for you must earn your keep."

When they returned home the old man congratulated his pupil. "You were a great success. There is something very special about the way you move, and the people respond to it." The cobra, of course, was delighted.

Each morning the cobra got into the basket, and gave many performances all over the city. Each night the snake charmer returned home with a purse jingling with coins. The cobra was famous now, but he was exhausted and had become thin with so much work.

One morning, as the old man was preparing the basket, the cobra said, "I shall give no more performances. I am leaving today."

"How is that?" said the old man incredulously.

"Now that I am famous," sighed the cobra, "all I do is work, work, work. At night I am so tired I can barely eat my supper. To tell the truth, I would rather be a simple cobra in the jungle than a famous one in a basket."

And he left.

·THE TIGHT SHOES·

Old Ahmed and his friend Ali had just finished their afternoon prayers. At the entrance to the Mosque they stopped to put on their shoes which had been left there in keeping with Moslem custom.

After diligently searching through the rows of shoes, Ahmed turned to Ali and said, "It seems someone took a fancy to the new shoes I wore today. They are not here. Would you kindly fetch me my old ones, which are at home."

"Of course," replied Ali. "I'll be as quick as I can. It's a pity about the new shoes, though," he added.

"On the contrary," Ahmed laughed. "I'm happy to see them gone. My wife gave them to me as a gift and they pinched my toes horribly. The thief did me a service. I only hope they fit him better than they fit me."